HOPE SPRINGS

For my friend, Henry, a gentle man who always had time to be kind. In December 2013, Henry passed on, leaving behind his wife, Ruth, his four children, his grandchildren and the orphaned children of Hope. He will be remembered. — E.W.

For Paul Layne — E.F.

Text copyright © 2014 by Eric Walters
Illustrations copyright © 2014 by Eugenie Fernandes

Published in Canada by Tundra Books, a division of Random House of Canada Limited, One Toronto Street, Suite 300, Toronto, Ontario M5C 2V6

Published in the United States by Tundra Books of Northern New York, P.O. Box 1030, Plattsburgh, New York 12901

Library of Congress Control Number: 2013953673

Library and Archives Canada Cataloguing in Publication

Walters, Eric, 1957–, author
    Hope springs / by Eric Walters ; illustrated by Eugenie Fernandes.

Issued in print and electronic formats.
ISBN 978-1-77049-530-2 (bound).—ISBN 978-1-77049-531-9 (epub)

    I. Fernandes, Eugenie, 1943–, illustrator II. Title.

PS8595.A598H67 2014   jC813'.54   C2013-906906-2
                                            C2013-906907-0

Edited by Debbie Rogosin and Samantha Swenson
Designed by Andrew Roberts
The artwork in this book was rendered in acrylic on paper.
The text was set in Zemke Hand.
www.tundrabooks.com

Printed and bound in China

1 2 3 4 5 6   19 18 17 16 15 14

HOPE
SPRINGS

written by
ERIC WALTERS

illustrated by
EUGENIE FERNANDES

TUNDRA BOOKS

"I can get there first!" Boniface called out, and a race was on. The children scrambled down the mountain path with their water containers.

Boniface put on a burst of speed, leaving the others behind in his dust! Then he heard little Mueni crying. Suddenly the race didn't seem important. As the biggest, he had to care for the littlest. Boniface stopped and waited. Mueni wasn't hurt, just afraid of being left behind . . . and alone. She'd spent so much time alone and afraid. Boniface knew what those feelings were like.

"No more tears," he said as he took her hand. "Little sister, you can walk with me."

Mueni wasn't really his sister, but all the children in the orphanage were like a family. And, as in all families, the children had chores to do. They worked hard, but nobody complained. At the orphanage, the children knew there would be food to eat, a bed to sleep in and houseparents to watch over them. For most of the children, this was the first time in their lives these things were certain.

Boniface and Mueni arrived at the spring and placed their containers at the end of a long line. This little spring was the only water for some distance. It was so small and there were so many people that it hardly seemed possible there would be enough water for everyone. But the water kept coming, drop by drop. Slowly it seeped from the rocks into a small muddy puddle, little trickles filling big containers.

There was always a long wait. The women used this time to talk. The children played. Mueni joined in a game, and Boniface's thoughts turned to his studies. His daydream was interrupted by a shout.

"Hey, what are you doing?" his twin brother Charles yelled as he raced toward the spring.

Two women had tossed the children's containers off to the side. Boniface ran to join his brother.

"Those are ours!" Charles said. "We have been waiting!"

"You are keeping *us* waiting!" one of the women snapped.

"You are not from here," a second woman growled.

"But we are!" Boniface said. He pointed to the top of the hill. In the distance, the little orphanage was visible through the trees.

"You may live here, but you are not from here," the first woman said. "This is *our* water for *our* families."

Boniface could not argue with an elder. He took his water container and placed it at the end of the line.

"No!" hissed the woman. "There is no water for you at all. You must leave!"

Boniface was frightened by the threats, the hard expressions and the angry staring eyes all around him.

"We must go," he said to the children. His lower lip trembled, but he knew he should not cry. As the oldest, he was the leader. They gathered their empty containers and left. The walk up the hill was going to be so much harder, weighed down with worry instead of water.

That night, Boniface couldn't sleep. They had brought no water, and he felt responsible. He tiptoed out of the bedroom he shared with the other boys and went to the kitchen where their houseparents, Ruth and Henry, were sitting.

"Not able to sleep?" asked Ruth.

Boniface shook his head. "I'm sorry about the water."

"There's nothing you could have done," Henry said. He had a gentle way with the children. He always had a smile to give or a hand to lend when theirs were too small to finish a chore.

"Is the well going to be ready soon?" Boniface asked.

A well was being dug at the orphanage. It was already so deep they could barely see the man digging at the bottom.

"We hope they will find water soon, but there are no guarantees," Henry said.

"What will we do until then?" Boniface wanted to know.

"Starting tomorrow," Ruth said, "some women will get water for us at night, when there is no lineup at the spring."

"I can go with them." Boniface was eager to help.

"You will be asleep," Ruth replied. "You need your rest, so you will do well at school."

Boniface hesitated. Then he asked softly, "Why were those people so mean to us?"

"What they did was not right. But it was not done out of meanness," Ruth explained. "It was done out of fear."

"Fear of what?" Boniface didn't understand.

"Because of the drought, they're afraid there will not be enough water for their families," Ruth said.

"They are so desperate for water that it is hard to be kind," Henry said. "And now, young man, it's time for sleep."

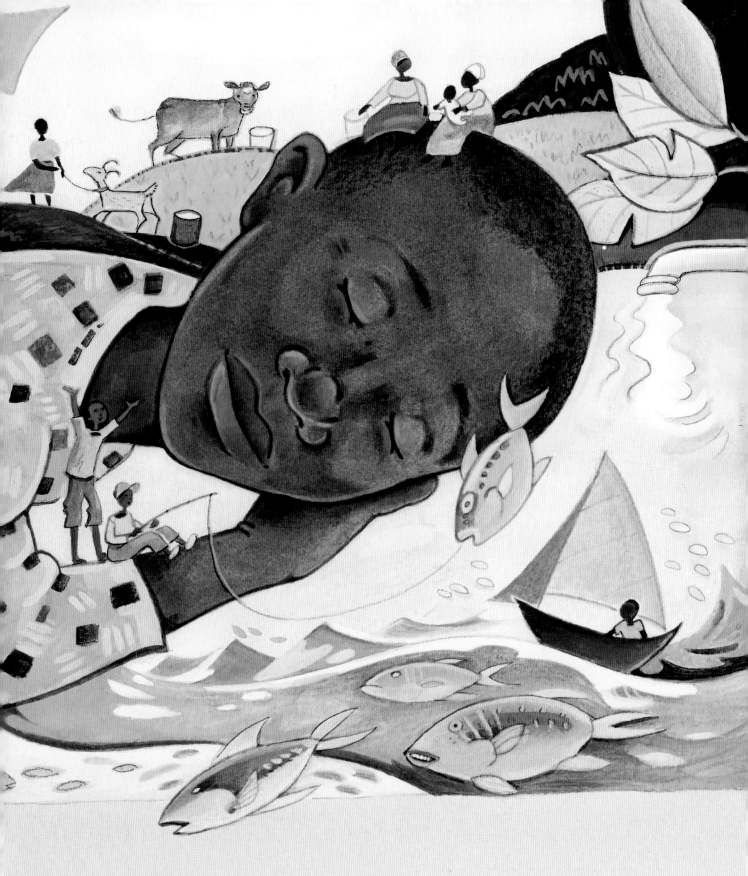

Boniface went back to bed. Soon he was dreaming of a place where there was enough water for everyone.

The next afternoon when the children got home from school, Boniface changed out of his school clothes and hurried to where the well was being dug. He'd done this every day since they had started, but today it seemed more urgent. One man sat waiting to haul up a bucket of soil being dug by his partner far below.

"Hello, little friend," the man said. "Are you here to ask your question again?"

Boniface nodded.

"Feel this," the man said, gesturing to the dirt in the bucket.

"It's wet!" Boniface was surprised.

"Yes, it is. The water is close now. Can you smell it?"

Boniface inhaled deeply. He *could* smell the water.

"You know," the man said, "when you have water, you have life."

Boniface was happy to help. Sometimes he moved the pile of dirt and chipped rock away from the edge of the hole. Today he would help haul up the bucket.

Suddenly there was a commotion. "*Maji, maji!* — Water, water!" the man yelled, his voice echoing up from the depths of the hole. Quickly he scampered to the top. Boniface could hear the water rushing into the well, filling it from the bottom.

THEY HAD WATER!

Over the weeks that followed, pipes were laid and the pump was connected. At each step, Boniface watched and helped. It was like a miracle. Now there was always enough to drink, and even after the crops were watered, the clothes washed and the children bathed, the well seemed to have no bottom; the water, no end.

Boniface stood by their wondrous well and looked down into the valley. Far below, through the trees, he could see the long line of containers waiting to be filled at the spring. The well had changed everything for the orphans, but the people in the valley were still desperate. It didn't seem right.

Boniface went to find Henry. He was working in the field.

"Could we talk?" Boniface asked.

"We can talk while we work — come and help." Henry handed Boniface a hoe
so he could weed while Henry picked tomatoes from the vines.

"Why the long face?" Henry asked.

"I was thinking about the water."

"Then you should be happy. Now we have all the water we need."

"Yes, but the people in the valley have so little." Boniface was thoughtful. "Do you think they could draw water from *our* well?"

"That is a generous offer, but while it is a giving well, it is not an endless well."

"Then could we dig a well at the spring?" Boniface asked.

"That is not so easy a job," said Henry.

"I watched and helped as our well was being dug," Boniface said. "And we have shovels, and some pipe and cement left over."

"You want to help the people who turned you away?"

"Yes," Boniface replied. "We are not desperate . . . so perhaps we can be kind. I know that when you give water, you give life."

Henry looked into Boniface's eyes. "I have always seen that kindness inside of you. We cannot do the work for them, but we can help them. Tomorrow we will speak to the people, and you will make your offer."

"Me?" said Boniface. "I wouldn't know what to say."

"You will know. Your words will flow from your kindness like the water will flow from the well," Henry said.

When the time came, Boniface *did* find the right words. With all the people working together, the little spring became a well. And there was enough water — and enough kindness — for all.

THE STORY BEHIND THE STORY

You've read the book. Now I'd like to tell you the story behind it.

Every summer, I spend time in the mountains of Mbooni District, Kenya, at the Rolling Hills Residence. Home to 52 orphans, it is part of the larger Hope Development program I founded with my wife, Anita, and Henry and Ruth Kyatha (www.creationofhope.com). The program also has over 40 students in residential high school and over 300 orphans residing in the community with extended family members. They are provided with monthly food packages, school fees, uniforms, bedding, livestock, tools and solar lanterns. In addition, the program runs a computer college, houses the only library in the area and funds and coordinates water projects.

Kenya and Mbooni District

Rolling Hills Residence

This area of Kenya is very dry. For water, all life depends on the twice-yearly rainy seasons, but they are not always reliable. Our water projects provide stable, regular sources of water not dependent on the rains. At one project opening an elder said to me, "You have not given us water, you have given us life." That statement is one of the most profound things ever said to me.

At the Residence we harvested water from roofs during the rainy seasons and stored it in large tanks. However, in 2010 a rainy season failed, leaving us with no water for our children or the farm. We had been planning for this — but our plans had not yet become reality. Two men with shovels and buckets were digging a well. They were 25 feet down and had not yet hit water — nor was there any guarantee that they would. While waiting for our well, we needed water.

Going to gather water is a fact of life in rural communities in Kenya. Our children were sent to the nearest water source, about a kilometer away at the bottom of the valley. Kyamutuo Spring was a trickle of water that dripped out of the rocks, pooling in a small muddy depression. It was the only source of water for 800 people — for drinking, for cooking, for their livestock and for irrigating crops. It was neither clean nor plentiful, but it was the only water available.

People waiting for water at Kyamutuo Spring.

Children gathering water at Kyamutuo Spring.

Children with their water containers

Bringing water back up the hill

Eric and the unfinished well at Rolling Hills

As the drought went on, the lineups at the spring lengthened. There could be 25 containers waiting in line, each one taking up to ten minutes to fill.

Our orphans come from across Mbooni District. Somebody in the line objected to their gathering water, saying, "You may live here now, but you are not from here!" They were threatened and forced to leave.

Our children were upset and troubled by the way they had been treated. Ruth and Henry explained that desperation causes even good people to do bad things — that these people were trying to protect their own children. This wasn't to excuse what happened, but simply to explain it.

But we were also desperate for water. We paid to have water brought in by tanker truck and hired adults to go to the spring at night — when the water simply drained away — as digging continued for our well.

At 30 feet down, the men hit a rock the size of a car. With hammer and chisel it was chipped through. The digging continued until finally, at 69 feet below the surface, water was struck. The Dawber Well — named after one of our donors — is a "giving well." It provides water for all the needs of our residence and farm. For our children, water was no longer an issue. But what about the people in the valley?

We sat down with the children and discussed what we could do. It was decided that we needed to talk to the people in the valley about a water project. Ruth and Henry met with them to negotiate a partnership. We would provide cement, steel rods and expertise. They would provide gravel, sand and labor.

In July of 2013 the water project was opened. Clean, plentiful water now flows from Kyamutuo Spring — Hope Springs. A 5-gallon container can be filled in less than a minute. No waterborne diseases have been reported. At night, the water collects in a pond. At dawn, it is opened up and the water flows through earthen canals to irrigate the crops of people in the community.

The partially completed well at Kyamutuo Springs

The new Hope Springs well

Mutuku singing at the Hope Springs opening ceremony

Charles, Mueni and Boniface

Ruth and Henry

Eric reading *Hope Springs*

Boniface, his twin brother, Charles, and Mueni are real. They are three of the
wonderful children who live at the Rolling Hills Residence. The story was told
through the eyes of Boniface and reflects the caring person he really is. He
loves the story and is thrilled to be the main character!

Eric Walters Autumn 2014